PUPPY SUMMER

PUPPY SUMMER

by

Meindert DeJong

Pictures by Anita Lobel

Harper & Row, Publishers   New York

To Patricia McElwee, my daughter-in-law,
because anyone who can at all times be
both gay and understanding deserves
my most appreciative dedication

Contents

PUPPY SUMMER

I
Turn Left—Turn Right

"It's the third little side road from here," Grandpa told Jon. "Turn to your right when you get there. Then follow your nose, and the second house you come to on the left side of the road, that's where they have three little puppies to give away. You'd better hurry—they won't last. 'First come, first served,' they said. It's a yellow house."

"What does that mean?" Jon asked. " 'First come, first served'?" He wanted to go quickly, but he was curious about the saying.

"It means, if you get there first, you get the pick of the lot and you can pick the one you like best."

"But won't I like them all?" Jon asked. It was hard to imagine you could like one puppy better than another, and then there still would be a third to choose from. He sighed. It was an anxious business—exciting but anxious.

He could hardly stand still to wait for Grandpa's answer. "If I take Vestri with me," he asked, "can she pick the best of the two after I pick the best of the three?"

"Yes, and if I'd go along too," Grandpa joked, "I could have the third and we'd have all three."

"Yeah," Jon yelled. "Yeah, Grandpa, you come along too. Then we'll have three puppies."

He yelled so loud that Vestri playing tea party with her three dolls on the front porch heard him. She came running.

"There's nothing like being a little bit greedy," Grandpa said to Jon. "But I'm afraid I can't come; I've got to milk the cow. However, you may take Vestri along but pick only one puppy between the two of you. One's enough, two's too many, and three's unheard of. Your poor grandmother is going to have her hands full as it is, housebreaking the puppy."

"What's 'housebreaking'?" Vestri asked breathlessly. She always spoke breathlessly. That was because she was always in such a hurry to ask questions, she didn't take time enough to breathe.

"What's 'housebreaking,' Grandpa?" Vestri asked again, without a single breath between the two questions.

"Well," Grandpa said, scratching his head under his hat. "Dogs—puppies don't wear diapers, you know, so it's the

[4]

rug that gets it. Grandma won't like it a bit—all that stooping and cleaning up after the pup. Two lively kids like Jon and you are quite enough for your grandma. I should have kept still about those puppies."

"Jon and I, we're housebroken," Vestri told Grandpa seriously, "so we can both help Grandma housebreak the puppy. But where is the puppy?"

"Third little side road from here, turn to your right," Grandpa said patiently again. "Then follow your noses, and the second house you come to on the left hand side, that's where they have puppies to give away. But only one! One. I'd better go prepare your grandma for what's going to happen to her."

Grandpa sounded so doubtful, Jon and Vestri were afraid that before they could get out of the long lane to the road, Grandpa would call out after them, "None. Do you hear? I changed my mind, so it's not one, it's none."

Jon and Vestri ran to get out of sight before Grandpa could change his mind, and to get out of hearing before he could reach the house to tell Grandma. What if Grandma said, "None. Not a one. Not a puppy."

Then they wouldn't have to run anywhere at all. Now they felt as if they could run over a hill or a mountain or even through a swamp without getting lost.

It turned out that Jon and Vestri did not need a swamp to

get lost in. They got lost on the road. They came to the third side road, when Vestri said in a small voice, "I don't know which is right or which is left."

It was because Vestri was left-handed. It always mixed her up.

"Which is right?" she asked her brother.

"Oh, that's easy," Jon told her. "You just make a writing motion with your hand—make believe you're holding a pencil—and that's your right hand. Then that's the right side, and the other is the left."

"Oh, Jon, that's an easy way to tell." Vestri grabbed a stick from the road, but she didn't just make-believe write. She wrote the word PUPPY. She wrote it in such big dust letters that the word almost crossed the whole road.

"That was an easy way to tell," Vestri said again as she threw the stick down on the dust word PUPPY. Then they both ran down the third little dirt road to get the real puppy.

Both had forgotten that Vestri wrote with her left hand! So they turned left down the third road instead of right as Grandpa had told them. They followed their noses but they followed them wrong.

There were only two houses and neither was yellow. And then there were no houses at all.

Soon after there were no houses, there was no road. The road became a wagon trail, the wagon trail became a cow path,

and the cow path led into a field of grass. The field of grass
went down a hill and became a swamp. The swamp was wet
and watery, and thick with huckleberry bushes. At the edge of
the swamp on his high stilt legs, higher than the bushes, stood
a big blue heron fishing for frogs. Vestri thought he was as tall
as she would be if she stood on Jon's shoulders.

The big heron was standing as still as the bushes and as still as the water. Then he heard Jon and Vestri come running down the hill. He squawked out in alarm, spread his great blue wings, and sailed out over the swamp and the water.

Then, of course, Vestri and Jon knew they had gone the wrong way. They knew that in a still and silent swamp where a heron fished for frogs and little fishes there could be no houses and there could be no puppies.

Vestri said, "Oh, Jon, I'm left-handed, so we turned wrong."

"Yes," he said slowly. "We sure did."

They turned around and started back up the hill. The heron sailed squawking over the swamp as if he were laughing at them.

The heron made Vestri laugh. "We almost came home with a big blue heron instead of a puppy," she said.

They both laughed, but they felt a little foolish just the same, and they trudged up the hill as if they were tired.

When they got to the top, Jon said, "Let's not tell anybody about it."

"No!" Vestri said. "Not even Grandma!"

Then they both felt better. In fact, they ran all the way back to the crossroad where Vestri had written the big dust word PUPPY across the whole road with her left hand.

2

Three's a Crowd

There stood Grandpa at the crossroad. They had said they weren't going to tell anybody about their mistake—but there stood Grandpa, right where Vestri had written the word PUPPY. He wasn't looking at the word; he was looking everywhere except the way from which they were coming.

Then Grandpa heard them running. He turned right around and called out, "Hola and hello, and welcome back, strangers. Grandma got worried you'd get lost, so she sent me out after you. She said she'd milk the cow. Well, I got to the yellow house and while there were a lot of yelping puppies there, there were no children at all. So I went back, but all I found was the word PUPPY here in the road."

Neither Jon nor Vestri could admit they had been lost. The

silence grew and finally Jon said, "There was a big heron squawking and flapping his wings in the swamp."

"Well, what was he flapping and squawking about?"

"It sounded as if he was laughing," Vestri said.

"Well, what was he laughing about?"

Grandpa grinned at her and Vestri grinned back, then in a little rush she admitted, "I guess he was laughing at me because I'm left-handed, Grandpa."

"And so that's how you discovered the swamp—by being left-handed," Grandpa said.

That was a nice way for Grandpa to put it.

"Did you discover the little lake in the middle of the swamp?" Grandpa asked.

"No-o-o," Jon and Vestri said together.

"Well, I must take you there someday to fish. It's full of little fish. Almost more fish than water."

"When can we go?" Jon demanded.

"Yes, Grandpa, when?" Vestri asked.

"Why, right now," Grandpa said innocently, "if you'd rather go fishing than go for a puppy."

Sometimes too much happened all at once.

"I thought you were going for a puppy," someone said right behind them. "Or are they all gone?"

It was Grandma leading the old cow by a long rope. "I do

declare," Grandma said, "our poor old cow is almost dry. I thought I'd stake her out in this tall grass. It took no time to milk her—I hardly got a cupful. Maybe enough for milk in our coffee in the morning, but I don't know what the children will put on their cereal."

"They'll just have to have coffee on their cereal," Grandpa said. He sounded very cheerful and as if he didn't much care. "The children want me to take them fishing," he told Grandmother.

"No, Grandma," Jon yelped. "We were going to the puppies. Will you go with us and help us pick one?"

"I'll come along to look," Grandmother said, "but nobody can pick out your puppy for you."

It wasn't hard to find the house with the puppies. They didn't even need to know the house was yellow, or that it was on the left side of the road. They could hear the puppies yelping far across the fields.

Then they were at the yellow house. All the way from the road they could see the three puppies in the doorway of a little barn. And the puppies saw them. If they had yelped before, they really started shrilling and yipping and wailing and crying when they saw Grandpa and Grandma and Jon and Vestri come toward them down the long driveway.

A little frame with foot-high chicken wire had been placed

across the open doorway to keep the puppies in the barn. But when the puppies saw four people coming toward them, they tried to climb and scramble over the screen.

The first one clambered and pulled himself up, then another puppy tried to pull itself up right over the first one, and they both fell down on their helpless, fat, broad backs. There they lay, all four legs kicking and pawing up from their round, tight, little milk bellies—as if they were swimming on their backs. But when the two that had fallen did get back on their feet, they immediately tried to climb over the third little puppy, and down went all three, flat on their backs, legs swimming in air.

When they saw that, Jon and Vestri couldn't stay with Grandmother and Grandfather—old people were far too slow. They charged down the driveway, stooped over the wire, and each grabbed a puppy.

The puppy left alone on the floor set up such a lonesome, forlorn howling, Vestri ran with her puppy to Grandmother, then rushed back to pick up the leftover, wriggling puppy and held him in her arms.

Grandfather stood by for a while and looked at all three of them with puppies in their arms. At last he said, "Now as soon as you children can calm yourselves, you'll have to pick out one puppy for your own."

[12]

It was impossible. Jon and Vestri looked from one puppy to the second, to the third, and back again. Vestri handed her puppy to Grandfather so she could see all three. She ran from one to the other. She reached up, she jumped up to look at the puppies in Grandpa's, Grandma's, and Jon's arms. She did it again and then still once more, and after all that she still couldn't decide.

Vestri got so desperate she pulled Jon's puppy out of his arms and said, "I'll hold him. You choose—you pick one puppy."

Then Jon did the same dashing that Vestri had done, running from one to the other and stretching up to look. But after all that he could no more decide than could Vestri. He finally told Grandma, "You do it. You decide, Grandma. I can't."

"Oh, I'm no better than you," she said. "When I pick one, I want the other. I end up by wanting all of them."

"Only one," Grandpa said sternly. "I said from the first— only one."

"Then *you* pick only one," Grandmother said impatiently, and put her puppy back behind the screen.

"Oh, no, oh, no," Grandpa said, putting his puppy back. "You don't catch me deciding. I'd never hear the end of it."

Then the puppy in Vestri's arms squealed and wriggled to be with the other two, so she put him behind the screen with the others.

[14]

They all four stepped back to look at the three puppies.

"Since none of us can decide," Grandma suggested, "let's let the woman of the house decide for us."

"She isn't home," Grandfather said. "When I got here earlier, looking for Jon and Vestri, she was just going to town. She said everything had been sold except one cow and her spin-drier washing machine. And, of course, the three puppies she was giving away. We were just to pick out any one of the three."

"What will we do now," Jon asked anxiously, "if the lady can't pick one for us?"

"I know," Vestri sang out. "We go, eeny, meeny, miney, mo."

Jon tried. But now, behind their wire screen, the puppies were trying to get out. They were jumping, scrambling, and climbing. They were falling and kicking in the air. Not one of them stayed still long enough to tell which was Eeny or Meeny or Miney or Mo.

"All right," Grandpa finally said. "Enough is enough. I'll close my eyes, reach over the fence, and whichever I pick— that will be our puppy."

As Grandpa said it, he did it. He scooped up one of the three, turned around, and walked down the long driveway, straight to the road. Grandma, Jon, and Vestri followed him. But the crying of the left-behind puppies was pathetic.

[15]

And the one in Grandpa's arms cried just as hard as the others.

"Oh, I can see this is going to be awful," Grandma said. "All his little life with the other two, and now in our big house alone. Are we doing right by just taking this one?"

"Well, then, take two," Grandpa said so promptly that it surprised Grandma, Vestri, and Jon.

Jon gave Grandpa no chance to change his mind. He flew to the little barn and grabbed up another puppy. He came running back with it tight in his arms.

But then it was twice as awful to hear the last left-behind puppy crying alone.

"Oh, listen to him. If that isn't a heartbreak," Grandmother said. "We can't do that, can we? Leave the little tyke in an empty barn all alone?"

"Well, if we take him that will make all three," Grandpa said. "I suppose three is no worse than two."

Vestri flew to get the last left-behind puppy.

When Vestri caught up with the others, the puppy hugged in her arms, Grandmother looked at it most doubtfully. "Goodness," she said, "what is the matter with us? I can see now that we shouldn't all have come. Now we've ended up with three yelping puppies."

"You were the one," Grandfather pointed out. "None of

the rest of us said anything about wanting all three."

"Three puppies," Grandmother said weakly. "What was the matter with my head?"

"It's not your head; it's your heart," Grandpa said. "And it's not merely three puppies. It's three puppies, one cow, and an almost brand-new washing machine with a spin-drier. The puppies are for Jon and Vestri, the cow is for me since our cow is going dry. But the washing machine is for you. It's to make your life easier now that you're going to have three lively young puppies with two lively young children in one house."

Then Grandmother was stern. "The wool has been pulled over my eyes," she told Grandfather. "Out with it. What have you been up to?"

Grandfather, chuckling, had to admit it all. "When I was here earlier, Mrs. Lewis told me she had sold everything but the cow and the washing machine, and she hadn't been able to give away the three puppies. She had sold their mother to a man in New Jersey. So there she was with three motherless puppies. And then I thought that with our old cow going dry we certainly needed a new, young cow. And you needed a washer with a spin-drier. Mrs. Lewis said that if I'd buy the cow and take all three puppies off her hands, she'd drop ten dollars on the cow. But if I'd buy the cow and the washing machine, and still take all the puppies, she would drop twenty-

[17]

five dollars on the cow and the washer. And there we are—with a cow, a washer, and three small dogs that saved us twenty-five dollars."

"There we are," Grandmother said slowly right after Grandpa. "Well, there we are, children. If your grandfather isn't the sly one! He had it all figured out, and all the time he had us picking and choosing one of the puppies, it was already all fixed up."

Then Vestri carried one puppy, Jon carried one, and Grandmother carried the third. Grandfather led the new cow. But the washing machine was left standing on the railingless porch of the yellow house.

3
Smith, Brown, and Jones

As they went down the road with the cow and the puppies, the new cow became stubborn. Grandpa pulled and tugged at her, but she wouldn't budge. Grandmother gave her puppy to Jon and went to help. But just then the new cow saw the old cow staked out in the grass, and from being stubborn she suddenly became eager. Instead of Grandpa pulling the cow, the cow now pulled Grandpa. She trotted away with him.

Grandma came on behind them, empty-handed. She had nothing. Her left-behind washing machine stood on the porch of the yellow house. It didn't seem right to Jon. He and Vestri had the puppies, Grandpa had the cow, but Grandma had nothing at all.

With his two puppies Jon started to run after Grandma. Grandma turned when she heard Jon coming, and Jon shoved the two puppies into her arms. There stood Grandma, two puppies in her arms, both wriggling and squirming and licking her face. Jon ran away to where Grandpa was tying the new cow to a fence close to the old cow so they could get acquainted.

From way back Vestri and Grandma could see Jon talking to Grandpa. Then Jon and Grandpa came back down the road, but they hurried right past without saying a word. They went back to the barn where the puppies had been. When they came out they had an old, red express cart.

Only Jon had seen the express cart hanging by a spike from the wall behind the puppies, and Jon had remembered.

He and Grandpa disappeared from sight behind the yellow house. After a while they appeared in the driveway, and when they turned into the road, Grandma and Vestri could see that Jon was pulling the express cart and Grandpa was steadying the washing machine that he and Jon must have lifted into the cart from the porch.

Vestri and Grandma stood waiting for them, struggling with the wriggly puppies in their arms.

When Jon and Grandpa came up to them, Grandpa lifted the cover off the washing machine, took the puppy out of Vestri's arms and put it down on the shiny, slippery bottom. It seemed such a good idea that Grandmother lowered her two puppies inside the washing machine.

Grandfather said to Grandmother, "Jon decided that if they

were going to have the puppies and I was going to have the cow, you should have your washing machine—right here and right now."

Grandmother beamed. She even blushed a little, she was so pleased.

Jon and Vestri pulled the cart, Grandma and Grandpa walked one on each side of the washing machine and steadied it, and the three puppies rode inside.

It was a sight. Inside the machine the puppies scratched, scrambled, and clawed, trying to climb up the smooth, white, rounded enamel walls. But always before they could stretch very high, they would slide down on their chins and skid on their round bellies on the bottom of the washing machine. Then they would try again. The puppies were so busy that for a while they forgot to whine. But then they saw Grandpa's and Grandma's faces above them and they immediately began to beg, yelp, and shrill and whine. It sounded terrible coming out of the hollow, deep, metal washing machine.

It was such a racket that Grandpa had to shout to make himself heard. "Listen! Listen!" he shouted to Grandma. "If you take the small cover off the spin-drier, I'll hold the big cover of the washing machine, then you can bang your cover against my cover and we'll be a circus."

To his surprise, Grandma grabbed the two covers and banged them together.

[21]

It made Jon and Vestri laugh so much, they could hardly pull the cart. It was fun. Besides, there was no one to see them except the two cows, and they were busy looking each other over.

It took a long time to bring the washing machine home this way. It was evening before they got to the long lane that led from the road to Grandfather's farm. It was getting dark inside the washing machine. The three puppies, tired from scrabbling and sliding, had fallen asleep.

They slept all the rest of the way home, no matter how much the express cart jolted and rattled over the ruts of the lane. Grandma put the big cover back to make it darker inside the washer, but she kept her hand under the edge so the puppies would get enough air.

"Ah," she said, "it's been a big day for them."

"It's been a big day for all of us," Grandpa said as they arrived at the porch of the farmhouse. "But now a big heave and a ho, and we're done."

So with Grandma and Grandpa on two sides of the washer and Jon and Vestri on the opposite sides, they managed with all of them lifting, struggling, and grunting to get it up the three steps of the porch. Then they rolled it on its own wheels into the kitchen, with the three puppies still sleeping inside.

Grandma looked all around and selected a spot right next to the back door where she wanted the washing machine to stand. "At least, *it* can stay in the house," she said, pleased. "It's the one thing we brought home that's housebroken."

"That reminds me," Grandpa said, "I'd better bring the two cows into the barn. If they spend the whole night side by side, they ought to be used to each other by morning, and I can put them in the swamp pasture. The grass is still green around the edges of the swamp."

"In the swamp pasture?" Jon exclaimed. "Does that swamp where the blue heron was belong to your farm too, Grandpa?"

"Yes, and the little lake in the swamp. And a little boat on that lake—but not the blue heron."

Jon laughed. Vestri was just lifting the cover of the washing machine and on tiptoe was peering down at the sleeping puppies. When she heard Jon laugh, she went "Shhh!" to him.

But it was her sharp "Shhh" that woke the puppies.

They leaped up, yelping to be lifted out.

"Now you've done it," Jon said to Vestri.

"I didn't—*you* did, laughing so loud," Vestri shouted.

"Never mind," Grandma said sharply. "The puppies can make quite enough noise without you two adding yours."

Grandpa nodded and tiptoed out of the kitchen to get the cows. He held his hands to his ears. "Want me to take the puppies to the barn now?" he asked over his shoulder.

"Are the puppies going to sleep in the barn?" Vestri asked anxiously. She looked out of the window where the day was darkening into night. The big barn loomed black and somber over the barnyard.

"Well, where did you think they were going to sleep?" Grandma asked. "They came out of a barn. They're used to a barn."

"But this one is so big, so big and dark," Vestri said woefully.

"Big barn, little barn," Grandma said firmly. "I can tell you that if we keep them here in the house, not one of us will sleep all night." She motioned to Grandpa to go on his way.

Vestri started crying. She was heartbroken at the thought of the tiny puppies in the big dark barn.

And Jon stood behind the washing machine and looked down at the puppies.

[24]

"I thought you two liked the big barn. You love to play in the hay," Grandmother said.

"But not in the nighttime," Vestri sobbed. "Just in the daytime. At night it's black and scary."

Grandmother did not argue. "Later we'll see. Later we'll train them. But this first night away from their mother and home, they'll have to spend in the barn. They'll be unhappy, but they'd be just as unhappy in the house, and not one of us would sleep a wink. There's nothing we can do; we can't explain things to them."

Vestri turned her face to the wall and sobbed. Jon looked down into the washing machine. It sounded as if the washing machine were sniffling—big hollow sniffles.

"Believe me, Vestri," Grandma said. "I'll do what I can for them. I'll put them in a bushel basket half full of soft straw and right in the middle of the basket I'll put our old alarm clock wrapped up in a woolen skirt. And do you know what? All of them will snuggle up close around it because the ticking will sound like their mother's heart beating. In a few nights they will be used to it here and they will love their new home."

But to Vestri and Jon it still sounded awful that the little puppies had to sleep in a basket in the middle of the blackness of the big dark barn.

When Grandfather came back from putting the cows into the basement of the barn, Vestri and Jon ran to him, and

Vestri sobbed out what Grandmother was planning to do with the puppies.

Grandfather said, "I guess your grandmother knows best. She has brought up puppies before."

Then Vestri started crying so hard, and Jon stood before Grandfather, swallowing in such a forlorn way that Grandfather looked questioningly at Grandma. In the washing machine one puppy woke and began yipping. Then they all were wailing and shrilling at the tops of their high, sharp little voices.

Grandpa slapped his hands to his ears. He strode to the washing machine. "Eeny, Meeny, and Miney, you be still," he said in a deep voice.

Vestri whirled from the wall. "Those aren't their names! Everybody knows those aren't their names!" she flared at Grandpa.

Grandmother didn't like the names either. "You're right, Vestri," she said. "Grandpa might as well call them Smith, Brown, and Jones."

To everybody's surprise Vestri thought those names were wonderful. "Smith, Brown, and Jones," she repeated. Yes, those were the names she wanted for the puppies. Smith would be the one with more white than black. The one that was mostly brown was, of course, Brown. The one with more

[26]

black than white would be Jones. "Smith, Brown, and Jones," she said and nodded her head, very pleased.

Somehow, naming the puppies had made Jon and Vestri feel better. But it hadn't really changed anything.

Then Grandmother, with a glance at Grandfather, smiled and said, "Well, with names like Smith, Brown, and Jones, we can hardly put them in the barn. All right, Vestri and Jon, you win. The puppies will sleep in the house."

Everybody felt better. Grandfather hustled off to get a basket out of the barn and fill it with straw so they could hide the clock in it. Vestri brought an old sweater, and Jon brought a woolen shirt. They each wanted to give something of their own for the puppies.

But Jon and Vestri knew they had gone far enough with Grandma. They did not dare beg her to put the bushel basket between their two beds.

4

A Barn Is a Daytime Place

Vestri woke up in the middle of the night. She just had to see the puppies down in the kitchen. But when she ran past Grandpa's and Grandma's bedroom, the door was wide open, the light was on, but Grandpa and Grandma weren't in the room. She and Jon had been sleeping all alone in the house— Grandfather and Grandmother were gone!

Vestri raced back to her bedroom, but Jon was so sound asleep she couldn't shake him awake. She even pulled Jon upright in his bed. But there he sat, eyes tightly shut. Vestri shook him harder, but the moment she let go, Jon dropped down on the bed, still sound asleep. Vestri became so desperate she slapped Jon's cheek.

That slap at last woke Jon. He stared straight up at Vestri and said, "And what do you think you're doing?"

"Grandpa and Grandma are gone!" Vestri said. "The light is on in their room, but they're gone. . . . Maybe the puppies are gone, too."

Vestri didn't know why she'd said that, but the moment Jon heard it he jumped out of bed. Together they hurried down the stairs to the kitchen. The light was on in the kitchen too, but the puppies were gone—even their bushel basket was gone. Jon and Vestri looked at each other.

[29]

"Did they take them back where we got them?" Vestri said, aghast. "Maybe they didn't like them—maybe the puppies kept them awake."

"That's it!" Jon said hopefully. "The puppies kept them awake, so they took them to the barn in the bushel basket. Let's go look."

Vestri hung back at the thought of going to the big black barn in the night. But the house was so empty and still that it was frightening too. She saw a flashlight on the cupboard counter, and gave it to Jon. "Let's go," she urged.

Vestri grabbed one of her dolls that had been on the cupboard counter beside the flashlight, and ran after Jon. Behind him she stepped out of the lighted kitchen into the pitch-black night.

"Wait for me," she begged. "Please!" But she didn't feel safe until she'd grabbed the waistband of Jon's pajamas. She clung to it.

"Man, Vestri," Jon scolded in a hushed, hoarse voice, "don't be so scared."

"But I am scared," Vestri gasped. She clung to her doll with one hand; with the other hand outstretched she clung to Jon. She followed him closely across the yard.

Suddenly the flashlight shone its small pinpoint of light through the enormous hay doors that stood wide open, into

[30]

the big black cavern of the night barn. But wherever the flashlight ranged, the floor of the barn between the two huge haymows towering to the peaked roof was empty. Outside, the night lay dark and still. Inside the barn, everything was dark and still.

Suddenly there was a small sound in the stillness. It even scared Jon, until at last he whispered, "That was just the cows in the basement."

It wasn't the cows. It was Grandpa! He suddenly came up from the basement. He saw Jon with the flashlight. Vestri stood so close behind Jon, Grandpa did not see her.

"Are you looking for me?" Grandfather said. "I'm looking for Grandma, but she isn't in the basement. Possibly she's up in the haymow. Hey, that flashlight's a good idea—let's have it."

But to climb to the haymow Grandpa had to turn off the flashlight. As the light disappeared Grandfather seemed to rise up in the darkness—straight up in the air. It turned out to be the ladder leading to the hayloft. Grandfather started up the ladder. Jon and Vestri climbed up after him. Vestri scrambled so hard after Grandpa that at times she grabbed his heels instead of the rungs of the ladder.

"You're supposed to climb the ladder, not me," Grandpa said from up in the hayloft. Then he reached down and pulled Vestri up, and after her he pulled Jon up into the hay. He turned the flashlight over a huge mound of hay. At first hay was all they could see. Then behind a mound of loose hay appeared a pair of big eyes, blinking into the light. It was Grandma!

"What—what are you three doing here?" she asked.

"Looking for you," Grandpa said.

"And the puppies," Jon added so loud that it rang and echoed under the high roof beams of the barn.

"Yes, the puppies," Vestri said.

"Oh, my goodness," Grandma said. She tried to sit up, but the loose hay kept slipping and sliding from under her. "I guess I built the sides of our nest too high," she laughed. "But I didn't want the puppies to climb over and fall down to the floor of the barn."

Grandpa, Jon, and Vestri waded through the deep hay to Grandma. There she lay in a deep nest of hay with only a white pillow for her head and a shawl thrown over her nightgown. It was lovely and warm in the new-mown hay high up under the roof of the enormous barn.

Next to Grandma in a little row lay the puppies. They were snuggled so cozily and sleeping so deeply after the excitement of their big day, they didn't even hear all the talk above them.

Behind Grandma, at the back of the hay nest, stuck down in deep dents, stood three small, white, empty bowls.

Vestri was almost crying at the awfulness of Grandmother's

[33]

sleeping in the big dark barn. "Grandma, why are you sleeping here?"

Grandmother laughed. "Well, I'll tell you. There was no sleeping in the house with those three wailing puppies. They were crying high and low. One would start mournfully low, the next one would go higher, and the third one would shrill out higher still.

"But worst of all were the three of you. The puppies woke me up, but they didn't wake any of you. Their noise disturbed your grandfather just enough that he started rolling and thrashing and snorting. It got so bad that I had to put one hand on the floor to keep from going overboard. Then when the puppies stopped a bit to rest their throats, I could hear you two children. Jon must have been dreaming about that squawking heron, because he kept laughing so loud he sort of sounded like the heron. And right in the midst of the laughing, it sounded as if you, Vestri, were reading a long Sunday school lesson to your dolls."

"No, Grandma!" Vestri and Jon said almost together.

"Yes, Grandma!" Grandmother said. "And you three sleepers were the ones who wanted the puppies in the house. Well, I went down to the kitchen and made myself a cup of coffee and tried to keep the puppies quiet, but finally I told them, 'Sitting up all night is no fun for any of us. Why don't we all get some sleep?'

"So I threw a pillow on top of their basket, for me, and I put my old woolen shawl over my shoulder, dumped three little bowls in with the puppies, and then we went to the barn. First we went down to the basement where the cows were, because I figured the puppies had yammered themselves hungry. The new cow kindly gave us three bowls of warm milk, so we had a little milk party right here in the barn. When they had lapped all their milk, they were so warm and so sleepy that I dumped them all back in the basket and tied it over my shoulder with the shawl, climbed the ladder, dug a deep nest, and there we were—sound asleep until you three came blundering in."

"Hey," Grandfather said, "is that an idea! It's high time you two city children found out what fun it is to sleep in a barn in the new-mown hay. I'll get us some pillows and we'll join Grandma."

Vestri and Jon looked a little doubtful, but they said nothing.

Grandpa disappeared down the ladder and with him went the only light. Vestri snuggled as close to Grandma as possible. Jon sat down and whispered, "Oh, the hay is warm and soft, Vestri. It tastes sweet, too."

He was chewing on a stalk. It was the only sound in the barn until Grandma said sleepily, "It sleeps the way it tastes —you'll see. Hay sleeps sweet."

That is how it was in the morning. They slept so sweetly, so soft, so long, the people and the puppies, that the sun seemed a great red ball rolling in through the wide-open doors of the barn. It was the cool of the morning, but the whole barn was sweet and warm with hay. They all sat up and looked out of the doorway—out over the fields. Then, far away in the rose-red of the morning, the blue heron flapped down from the sky to the blue water of the lake.

They looked at each other and then down at the puppies, and almost together they breathed deeply and said, "Ah." At that sound the puppies woke up.

"Ah," Grandpa said. "Now we'll feel like living again through another day. Ah."

5

Hat with Holes

Grandpa came hurrying into the basement of the big barn where Jon sat doing nothing. It was too hot outside and too stifling everywhere else to do anything.

Having just come out of the glare of the afternoon sun, Grandpa peered about in the dim, cool darkness of the basement. "Oh, there you are—sitting still. Not sick, are you?"

Grandpa dug in his pocket, came over, and slid something into Jon's hand.

Jon glanced at the flat, three-cornered, stonelike thing and looked up at Grandpa, unbelieving. But it was! It was a real flint Indian arrowhead. The hot, dull afternoon became exciting.

"Oh," Grandpa assured him, "it's real, all right. They

fought all kinds of battles the length and breadth of this whole farm. Of course it wasn't a farm then; just a lake, a swamp, and an Indian village on the shore of the lake. Man, I even plowed up a whole skeleton one year right in the cornfield. And my father before me dug up one when he was draining a ditch on the edge of the swamp. Skeletons from men fallen in a long-ago battle, I guess. The one in the ditch had a spearhead between his ribs. I was just a kid then. Man, was I excited.

"But there's no end of arrowheads and spearheads and heads of axes and tomahawks all over this farm. It kind of looks as if that battle raged all the way from the swamp and the lake to what's now the alfalfa field behind that yellow house where we got the puppies."

Jon stared at the arrowhead, then he stared at Grandpa. Then he said slowly, "Grandpa. The whole summer is gone —the whole summer—and only now you tell me about the arrowheads and the Indians and the battles."

Grandpa grinned. "Wouldn't have thought of it now if it hadn't been such a hot day, and if I hadn't dulled my hoe on that arrowhead I just gave you. Well, I needed to fill my jug with fresh water again, anyway, so I thought while I was doing that I might as well get a file and sharpen the hoe. Go get the file for me, will you? It's up in the barn in that little harness room. Whew, it's hot. Where's Vestri? Where's Grandma? And where are the puppies? Who's taking care of them in this heat?"

Jon didn't answer. He rushed to get the file. Sometimes it was better to rush away and do something; otherwise you might say too much. Imagine, all the long summer Grandpa had never said one thing about arrowheads. Even whole skeletons! And now vacation was almost over. It would soon be time to go back to town and to school—an apartment and school.

Jon found the little room. It had a door that looked so much a part of the wall, except for a little knob like the knob of a dresser, that he had never noticed it before.

The room reeked of leather. All its four walls were hung full of leather things—straps, reins, belts with buckles, harnesses, and even a couple of saddles. High up on the wall Jon noticed an enormous straw hat. The hat had two holes in the brim. Not worn holes, not holes punched by the big nail from which it hung. Neat holes. Made holes; one on each side. It was as if they had been made for ears to poke up through.

Jon pondered the strange hat a moment, but the closed room was too stifling to stay there long. He grabbed the file from the bench and rushed back downstairs. He had intended to ask all kinds of questions about the Indians and about the big hat with the holes, but instead he blurted out, "Grandpa, may I go out over the farm right now to explore and look for Indian things?"

And Grandpa said just as quickly, "No. No, absolutely not. This must be the hottest afternoon of the hottest day of a whole hot summer. It's too chancy going out in the fields in this heat. You stay around the yard and keep in the shade. Yes, and see that the puppies are kept in the shade. By the way, who is supposed to be taking care of them—you or Vestri? Or are they with Grandma again?"

"I guess Vestri," Jon said.

He couldn't be bothered with Vestri and puppies right now. His mind was seething with big plans for hunting arrowheads and with questions about the Indian battles that had raged from the swamp to the potato patch right near the house. "If it gets cool tonight," he begged, "may I go and hunt for arrowheads and stuff—if I take good care of the puppies all afternoon?"

Grandpa raised his hands in mock horror. "If you take care of the puppies! Whose puppies are they? And here I thought they were yours and Vestri's. Let's see . . . how long have we had them? Just a little better than a week? And already it's become a chore to look after them?"

[41]

"But, Grandpa," Jon said. "In just another week the summer'll be over, and school will start, and we'll be going back home to Mother in town. And here I was all summer and you never told me about arrowheads. And now you won't even let me look. Grandpa," he asked in a hushed voice, "were those skeletons scalped?"

Grandpa just grinned. "There's a lot more summers ahead of you. You're not *too* old yet," he said, standing up and putting the hoe on his shoulder. "Meanwhile, stay cool, keep the puppies cool while I try it once more in the potato patch, which—if it gets any hotter—will be a fried-potato patch." Then, laughing, he calmly walked out of the barn without even answering Jon's question.

For a while Jon moped around in the dim basement, but that was dull. Suddenly he thought of the big hat. He raced up the stairs to the closed, stuffy little room.

It was awfully quiet in there. Outside, the yard was quiet, too—the whole farm was quiet. It almost seemed the deep quiet of long, long ago, except that then there had been Indians and battles, war cries and blood, and death and left-behind skeletons.

Jon wondered if he could reach the high hat from the top of the tool bench. . . . Hey, maybe in this barn, on this farm, there had once been not only Indians but a giant! This was his hat!

With a hard jump up from the top of the bench Jon knocked the hat to the floor, and came down after it. He hurried out, but once outdoors he had to stop and try on the big hat. It fell right down over his head and would have fallen to his shoulders if his ear hadn't come sticking through one of the holes at the side of the crown. It certainly was the hat of a giant. A little scared, Jon ripped it off.

Jon bolted like a wild colt across the yard to the corncrib

under the maple tree. He came rushing in to where Vestri was playing. Then it was sort of silly, for there she sat on the floor playing with dolls' hats.

She had ranged all her dolls' hats around her and was playing tea party. Of all the silly girls' games!

Vestri looked up from pouring make-believe tea for the doll hats.

"I found the hat of a giant," Jon said in a hoarse voice. He was breathing hard. "Boy," he said, "I'll bet he killed a lot of Indians in that big battle on this farm."

"Who?" Vestri asked. She looked from her dolls' hats to the big hat that Jon held up for her to see. "Why, it's no good," she said. "It's got holes in it."

"Of course there's holes in it," Jon told her. "Those were for the giant's giant ears."

Vestri's eyes opened wide. She shrank back from the hat when Jon held it out to her. She wouldn't touch it.

"It won't bite you," Jon said. But he put the scary hat behind him.

"Why are you playing with doll hats?" he asked scornfully.

Vestri shrugged. "Oh, I don't know," she said. "I guess because I couldn't find my dolls. It was too hot to go looking for them, so I made believe the hat was the doll."

Jon was amazed. "Can you do that? Really? Make believe a hat is a whole doll?"

Vestri nodded. She looked smart and mysterious.

Jon swept the big hat from behind him and dropped it in front of her. "Imagine the whole giant from the giant's hat," he ordered.

Vestri stared into the hat lying on the floor, but she did not say anything. It was quiet in the corncrib. In the trees insects shrilled. It sounded hot. "Aren't you taking care of the puppies?" Jon demanded.

"No," Vestri said. "You know very well you were supposed to. I did it this morning."

"Then who is taking care of them?"

"Grandma, I guess," Vestri said, but she wasn't paying much attention. She must have gotten over being afraid of the hat, for she had picked it up and was staring at Jon with one eye through one of the hat's holes. He wanted to hit her.

"Grandpa said there was a giant skeleton—two of them—found on this farm, right near here." There, that should scare her.

It did. Vestri dropped the hat. "Giant skeletons, real giants?" she quavered.

Jon shrugged. "Sure," he said. But inside he knew Grandpa hadn't said "giant" skeletons. He'd said "whole" skeletons. But "whole" had sounded big. "There was a big Indian battle," he informed Vestri. "There's loads of arrowheads and everything all over this farm. And if it weren't for those blasted puppies you and I could go right now and hunt for arrowheads in the swamp. Grandpa wouldn't see us there. It's over the hill. Maybe we'd even find a skeleton in a hole in the swamp. Golly, what if we found the skeleton of the giant who used to own this hat, and there he was, scalped by the Indians and stuffed down a hole in the swamp. Golly."

Vestri kept backing away from him. Now she wouldn't go with him, and he didn't want to go alone—not even in the bright sunlight. "Aw," he said hastily, "I was just making that up about giant skeletons. We'll just look for arrowheads."

But Vestri was really upset. "What you said!" She looked at Jon with her Sunday-school look.

"What did I say?" Jon said indignantly. "Grandpa says 'golly'," he defended himself.

"No, but you said, 'blasted.'" Vestri's mouth was all pinched up as if her lips couldn't bear to touch the word.

"Well, Grandpa says 'blasted.'"

"But you said 'blasted puppies.' You don't even like them anymore. You don't take care of them when it's your turn. All you want to do is hunt old arrowheads."

"I don't either," Jon shouted, hurt and indignant. "I didn't even know about the arrowheads, so how could I hunt them? And you don't take care of the puppies either, unless Grandma makes you—so there!"

"I do too. And I clean up their messes. I don't just make a gaggy face like you do and run away," Vestri yelled back.

It was as if for a moment the insect shrilling stopped. They heard themselves shouting in the stillness. They both whirled around and looked out of the open door, half afraid Grandpa might be standing there listening to them. They looked toward the house—all the windows were open. . . . If Grandma heard! Then they saw the jug of water. Grandpa must have forgotten it. He must have left it standing in the shade, but

[47]

now the shade had moved on and the glass jug stood blazing white in the sun.

Jon and Vestri looked at each other. They knew they were thinking the same thing—that one of them ought to take the jug to Grandpa in the potato patch. Neither one of them moved. It was too hot. It was nice and darkish and shady in the slatted corncrib and sometimes there was almost a breeze —a little shifting of air through the open doorway.

"Oh, Grandpa forgot his water. We ought to take it to him," Jon said, feeling things out.

"He forgot it because he wanted to bring you that old arrowhead," Vestri said. "He asked me where you were and I told him, but then he forgot his water, so it's really you who should take it out to him."

Jon gave her a shrewd look. "All right," he agreed, "but then you've got to get the puppies for me and play with them till I get back." It seemed a smart bargain. Grandpa had said to stay out of the sun, but if he took the jug of water to him, that would be a good deed. And on the way to the potato patch and on the way back he would hunt for arrowheads, and Vestri would be taking care of the puppies.

Vestri outguessed him. "Sure," she said. "I know you— you won't come back. You'll go hunting old arrowheads and then I'm stuck with the puppies. I know you, Jon Langford."

"Well, you can't carry a gallon jug," Jon argued. "You're

a girl and I'm a boy, and besides, I'm older, and . . ."

"Grandpa will come to get the water when he gets thirsty," Vestri said comfortably and coolly. It sounded cruel and self-ish. Jon's mouth dropped open. Now it was his turn to say like a teacher, "Why, Vestri Langford, if your mother heard *you!*"

Vestri had seen Grandpa coming toward the yard from the potato patch, but Jon's back had been turned. Now, because of the queer expression on Vestri's face, he looked over his shoulder and he too saw Grandpa coming. Without another word he scooted to get the puppies out of the house. "All right for you, Vestri," he muttered to himself.

After Grandpa had filled his jug with fresh, cold water, he brought it over to the corncrib and had a tea party with Vestri. He sat on the floor beside her and poured the tea water; Vestri couldn't handle the gallon jug. Grandpa showed her how farmers did it, by swinging the jug to one shoulder and letting the cups "gutter full." He filled all the small tea-cups, not just two, and then he greedily drank from all of them. "Never have I known such a thirst," he said, and grinned when he saw Vestri's amazed face.

Vestri swallowed her surprise, shoved herself a little closer to the cups, and said in her best tea-party voice, "Jon just left here to get the puppies and bring them to the party."

"Yes, I saw him scoot when he saw me coming," Grandpa

[49]

said. "Man, was it dry in that potato patch. I must say, Vestri, you've done yourself proud. You have certainly found the coolest spot on this farm." Grandpa swung the jug to his shoulder and filled the cups again. "Best pump-water tea party I've ever been to," he said. "Now I don't know whether this is a proper matter to bring up at a tea party, but it seems to me that since the puppies arrived there's no care been taken of a certain girl's dolls. The other day I came across what

Grandma says is called a 'wetting' doll lying sprawled on its face on the floor of the barn. I'm glad to say that when I picked it up it didn't wet, but it did say 'Mama' to me very nicely. I guess that doll is still sitting up on the beam where I put it. But it also seems to me that lately there is rather poor care being taken of the puppies."

"Grandpa," Vestri said earnestly, "since the three puppies came and I have to clean up after them when they wet, why would I want to play with a doll who wets some more? And, Grandpa, I do take care of the puppies in the morning. Jon is supposed to look after them in the afternoon."

"I see. Wetting dolls and wetting puppies—you don't need both." Grandpa choked on the water he was drinking. He turned around and saw the giant hat lying in the corner. "What's that doing here?" he managed to sputter.

"Jon brought it," Vestri said. "Jon said it belonged to a real giant. He's going to look for the giant's skeleton in the swamp. The Indians scalped the giant."

Grandpa stared and then started to laugh. "Who made that up? Where did Jon hear all that? Why that's nothing but a hat for a horse! See the holes for the ears? My grandfather used to put hats on the horses when he was working them in the hot fields."

Vestri couldn't believe it.

"Honest, it's so," Grandpa assured her. "It kept the horses' heads cooler when they worked all day in the heat."

Vestri was thinking. Jon had deliberately scared her with his story of giants and skeletons. Jon liked to tease. Well, maybe she could pay him back. "Grandpa," she said, "couldn't we cut holes in my doll hats for the puppies' ears and tell Jon they were puppies that belonged to the giant? Anyhow," she coaxed, "wouldn't it make them cooler, too? Then they wouldn't have to stay inside all the time."

Grandfather chuckled. "Well, now, Vestri, I guess you can keep up with Jon, can't you? We can try doing it if you don't mind a few ruined doll hats. I'll make the holes for the puppies' ears with my jackknife."

"Let's hurry and do it before Jon comes back," Vestri said eagerly. She giggled at the thought of Jon's eyes when he saw the little flop ears of the puppies sticking out from the doll hats.

"Yes, Jon and his wild ideas. Hat that belonged to a giant! Let's teach him a lesson," Grandpa agreed.

Jon did not come back alone with the puppies. Grandma came with him. She was puzzled over Jon's story of a big hat that belonged to a giant. The puppies ran ahead to the corn-crib, and Grandpa grabbed them and pulled their soft little ears through the holes in the hats, and tied the hat ribbons under their little chins.

Grandma was still puzzling about the giant's hat when she and Jon got to the corncrib. Jon picked up the big hat and gave it to her. "See?" he said. "See, I told you, didn't I?"

"Why, Jon," Grandma answered, "that's a hat for a horse." Then Vestri and Grandpa pushed the three puppies, with their silly-looking hats on their heads, toward Jon and Grandma.

Vestri's giggle made them both turn around, and then they saw the puppies trying to paw the hats from their heads.

"Look, Jon," Vestri said. "Look, here are the giant's dogs. They wear hats too." She doubled up and held her stomach and giggled and giggled.

Grandpa stood chuckling too. Jon's face fell. Then it turned bright red. He looked miserable. He did not think it one bit funny. Grandma felt sorry for him. She decided she did not like the joke either.

"I was going to ask you to get me a pail from the pump, Jon," she said. "But I don't think I want to sit on an upside-down pail at this tea party. I don't like this party—I don't like the people. I don't think they are nice at all, and certainly they are not funny. Come on, let's go out and hunt for arrowheads along the lane where it's shady."

With her chin up high and haughty Grandma walked straight out of the corncrib. She and Jon strode away. Then out of the door, right after Grandma, tumbled the three puppies in their bright-colored hats. In single file they followed Grandma and Jon down the lane.

"All right. We're sorry," Grandpa called after them. "Vestri and I will hunt arrowheads for Jon too. . . . Hey, we'll make it a contest and see who will find the first bushel basketful. And the one who finds the least has to wear the horse's hat—with his ears pulled through."

Jon and Grandma did not bother to answer. But they had the last laugh. When Grandpa and Vestri set off in the opposite direction, the puppies turned and waved their questioning tails, stared at them, and then turned back to stay close to Grandma and Jon.

Suddenly Smith, Brown, and Jones sat down, looked at each other, and began to eat each other's hats.

6

Corncrib Court

It was late in the afternoon, and even hotter than yesterday and the day before. The nights in between were equally hot. Night and day the air was so still and motionless it seemed almost impossible to breathe. Just when the puppies were beginning to keep quiet most of the night, nobody could sleep because of the heat.

"That's dog days for you," Grandpa called out across the yard as he left for the potato patch. "The meanest days of the whole summer, and it's a good thing dog days come at the end of summer because soon after comes fall."

"Yes, fall and school," Vestri piped up from the corncrib where she was reading. "Those are dog days for us. These are just nice puppy days."

"Mighty hot puppies," Grandpa said, grinning. He moved slowly out over the yard toward the potato patch.

From where he sat in the shade of the stone wall of the barn, Jon looked up from his book, opened his mouth to say something about dog days, but he closed it again. It was even too hot to ask questions. He did not seem to want to know anything. He went on reading in the shade. That was what the weather was good for—for reading a book.

It seemed to both Jon and Vestri from their different reading spots that Grandpa had only just left for the potato patch, but there he stood in the yard again. He came toward the shade of the barn. "I give up," he told Jon. "It's just too hot to work. A man accomplishes nothing anyway in heat like this, and he risks the chance of sunstroke, heat prostration, the megrims, and maybe even measles." He went into the barn, chuckling to himself. Neither Jon nor Vestri looked up from their books.

Moments later Jon closed his book. There was nothing to do—nothing but wait for supper, and then maybe after supper, when the sun went down, he could look for Indian arrowheads again. Jon hadn't found a single one since Grandpa had told him about the great Indian battle that had raged over the farm.

At that moment inside the house, in the kitchen, in front of the stove, Grandmother accidentally stepped on the paw of one of the puppies.

The stepped-on puppy wailed as if it were being whipped

within an inch of its life. The other two puppies began crying as if they, too, were being beaten.

Grandmother picked up the stepped-on puppy and felt its paw to see if it were broken. It seemed all right and she gave it a quick kiss. That helped, but now the other two puppies cried to be picked up and kissed too.

When the cries of the puppies came shrilling out of the house, it was as if a fire alarm had rung out over the farm. Vestri got to the kitchen first, but Jon and Grandfather came pounding hard behind her. They burst into the kitchen, tumbling through the screen door one after the other.

There they stood, side by side, without being able to utter a word, they'd run so hard in the awful heat. The screen door slammed shut by itself as the three stood heaving and panting. Grandmother slowly turned, stood with her back to the stove, facing the row of accusing eyes, with the three puppies who were quiet now in her arms.

"You'd think I'd murdered you," Grandmother said softly to the puppies. "You'd think I'd skinned you alive."

Then Grandma looked up. "Well," she said, "isn't that the way—the three of you stand there and accuse me with your eyes?"

Grandpa and Vestri and Jon were so surprised at the sudden outburst, they had nothing to say.

"All I did," Grandmother said, "was to step, purely by

accident, mind you, with my soft slipper on the tip of one of the paws of one of the pups. But I *didn't* do it on purpose! It was an *accident*. And I am *sorry*. Now will you all get out of my kitchen as fast as you came in? And take your dogs with you!" She shoved the puppies into their arms. She shoved the three of them—Grandpa too—right out through the screen door, out of the kitchen.

"Our *dogs?*" Grandpa tried to make a joke of it to put Grandma back in good humor. "You make them sound as big as Saint Bernards. Why I could hide all three under my one big foot."

It didn't work. It was too hot. The kitchen was like an oven. Grandma didn't even smile. She just tiredly pushed a damp strand of hair off her forehead. "That is exactly it," she said. "They get underfoot. Under my feet, every other step. The way they've grown in the week or so we've had them, they're not puppies anymore. They've become bowling balls. They don't run, they roll over my kitchen floor. They even sound like bowling balls. They're getting into everything."

Neither Grandpa nor Jon nor Vestri said a word.

"And just whose dogs are they?" Grandma demanded. "Mine? I don't know, but I've had the care of them again this whole hot afternoon. And that's the way it's been all week. And, may I ask, just what have you three been doing?"

Grandfather grinned, opened the screen door, and pushed

[59]

his puppy back into the kitchen. Then he strode off toward the barn. But Jon and Vestri clung to their puppies and peered through the screen door at Grandma.

Grandmother calmed down. She had been so angry because she had been scared by the yelping of the puppy she had stepped on. It was Jones that Grandpa had set back in the kitchen, and it was Jones who had been stepped on. He still kept putting his paw up for sympathy, and since he wasn't getting any from Grandma right now, he held it up before the screen door for Vestri and Jon and the other two puppies to see. Vestri felt so bad that while Grandmother was busy at the stove Vestri handed her puppy to Jon and worked the screen door open enough to pull Jones outside. She held him and hugged him tight. She started to cry.

Jon looked over his puppies at Vestri. "Boy, you're lucky you're a girl. You can cry. Boys aren't supposed to cry over little things like this."

"Jones didn't think it was a little thing—and you'd cry too, if you were a girl," Vestri said unreasonably.

Grandmother spoke through the door. "You children wanted the three puppies. You've got the three puppies but only one duty. Only one duty—keep them out from under my feet when I'm fixing meals. It's too dangerous."

"It isn't fair!" Vestri blazed out. She hadn't quite forgiven Grandma for stepping on Jones, even if it was an accident.

[60]

"Grandma, it isn't fair. Last week you said that cleaning up after the puppies was our only-one duty. And even then, I have to do it all. Jon makes a face as if he's going to gag, and so I have to clean it. And now you say keeping them out of the kitchen is my only-one duty too. And . . . and . . ."

"Well," Grandma said impatiently, "then it would seem you now have two only-one duties. See to it that you take care of them both."

"But what about Jon?"

Over his wriggling, hot armload of puppies, Jon glared at Vestri. He whispered as if into one of the puppies' ears, "*Tattletale!*"

"Jon! I heard that," Grandma said. "Well, here comes your grandfather. He can take care of you."

Jon turned around guiltily, and there came Grandpa carrying a huge, snakelike whip. But he strode right by them into the kitchen and held it out to Grandma. "I found this in the barn," he said. "Since I've no use for it, I thought you might use it to control those three great Saint Bernards."

"You," Grandma said, and then she could not help laughing. "You, Grandpa, are a goofball."

Vestri and Jon were so relieved to hear Grandma laugh that they laughed too—high and long. The puppies just looked astonished.

"No," Grandpa said. "That's not what I am; I'm a judge.

And our Corncrib Court is going to be in session right now. I heard a big quarrel going that stopped when I showed up with the whip. It's the heat! We're all getting too easily upset." Grandpa went to the oil stove and turned off the burners. "It's hot enough without making more heat. Let's get out of this kitchen and out to the corncrib. I discovered when we had our tea party out there that Vestri had found the coolest place on this farm. So now we'll hold court in there and settle our problems. I don't know, maybe afterwards we'll eat there. Come along, everyone, and bring the puppies. Jon, you fetch a stool for your grandmother. She can't sit on the floor like us roughnecks."

"My goodness gracious," Grandmother said, sitting flushed and pink-faced on the stool. "This is cool!" She reached up and took the big hat down from its nail above the door and sat there fanning herself with it. "It certainly is cool. Funny, but I didn't notice how cool it was the day you were making fun of Jon because of this hat." She suddenly stopped fanning herself and sat looking inside the big hat, and then she said to Vestri, "Run to the house and get me my sewing basket, but be sure to see if there's any elastic in it. Otherwise there'll be elastic in the top right-hand drawer of the sewing machine."

Everybody looked at Grandmother, very puzzled.

[63]

"Looking at this hat," she said, "and remembering your making fun of poor Jon, it suddenly struck me it's all right to have this Corncrib Court and talk out our troubles instead of letting them get us upset. But there also ought to be some punishment for the one we decide is the guilty one. The funnier and the more ridiculous the punishment, the better it will be. So I'll string elastic inside this hat, and in that way make it so it'll fit anybody. And the holes for the big donkey's, or mule's, ears are, of course, already in it."

Everybody thought that was a wonderful idea, and Vestri ran to get the sewing basket and the elastic.

When Vestri came panting back, Grandpa sat down in the narrow doorway. "This Corncrib Court is now in session," he said. "A little silence, please."

Grandma sat on the stool, busily stringing elastic inside the big horse's hat.

"All right, Vestri, I heard you complaining a while back at the kitchen door that something or someone wasn't fair," Grandfather suddenly said from the doorway. "What or who isn't fair?"

For a moment Vestri shrank back, Grandfather had come out with it so directly and so suddenly. Then turning a bit pale, she stood up and said right out, "Grandpa, I think it's Grandma that isn't being fair."

[64]

"Me!" Grandmother said, astounded. She almost rose up from her stool in indignation.

"Silence in this court. Vestri has the floor," Grandfather ordered. Grandmother sat down again.

"I guess it is this heat," she said thoughtfully. "I guess one puppy would have been more than enough, but in this heat three turned out to be a disaster."

Vestri stepped right up to Grandmother. "Grandma," she said sternly, "one puppy is not enough and it's a good thing there are three, because if there was only one, Jon and I would love it to pieces; so three is just enough."

"Wait a minute," Grandpa said. "Wait a minute. That's a fine speech, but I heard Grandma bawling you out for not taking care of the puppies. Of course, loving them is easy; it's the caring for them that's the work."

Little Vestri stood there. She put her hands on her sides and stuck out her elbows. "That's exactly what isn't fair! Last week Grandma said our one duty was to clean up after the puppies. Later she said our one duty was to see that they didn't play too hard in the heat. Then our one duty was to see that there was always plenty of water or milk standing out for them. But now, today, she said that our one duty was to keep them out of the kitchen."

Grandfather rubbed his hand over his mouth and looked at

[65]

Vestri most soberly. Jon looked in amazement at his fiery little sister. He thought that in all her life she had never said anything so right and so smart.

Grandfather turned to Grandmother. "I see you've fixed the horse's hat so it will fit any of us. Well," he said slowly, "if what Vestri said is right, maybe you should put it on."

Grandmother smiled. "Maybe she is a little bit right. I guess I do forget the next day what I've said the day before. Yes, she is right—that certainly does make a lot of 'one' duties when you put them all together like that."

Without another word Grandmother put on the horse's hat.

Vestri jumped up and snatched it from Grandmother's head. She got very red in the face. She didn't like it at all, her grandmother wearing a horse's hat. "Grandma," she said, "that isn't the part that is unfair. That isn't what I meant. What isn't fair is that all those 'one' duties are all *my* duties, and not Jon's."

"Aha, Jon," Grandfather said. "Now things have moved over to you. It looks like you're to wear the horse's hat. When you do, be sure to pull your ears way through the holes."

"Yes, he should!" Vestri said, and she slammed the hat right down over Jon's head.

Jon indignantly ripped the hat off his head. But Vestri stood pointing her finger at him. "Grandma and Grandpa!

[66]

Last week Jon and I decided I'd take care of the puppies in the mornings, and he would take care of them in the afternoons. Then this week we'd turn it around."

"Jon, stand up." Grandfather said. "Is what Vestri just said true? Did you decide that?"

Jon slowly nodded.

"Did you do it?"

Jon said nothing.

"Well, who took care of the puppies this afternoon?"

"I guess Grandma," Jon said in a small voice.

"And yesterday afternoon?"

"I guess Grandma."

"And the afternoon before that?"

"I guess Grandma."

Grandfather turned to Grandma. "It sounds to me like this boy, Jon, is doing some accurate guessing. What do you think?"

"Very accurate. I see an awful lot of the puppies in my kitchen every afternoon, but I see mighty little of the boy, Jon."

"Well, now who gets to wear the horse's hat?" Grandpa asked. "You, Jon, for shirking your duties, or you, Grandma, for letting him get away with it?"

"It looks like we ought to take turns," Grandma said as she reached for the hat.

"No!" Jon said. "Not Grandma." He held the hat away from Grandma, but he did not put it on his own head.

[68]

Grandpa stood looking at him. "Well, then, maybe I should wear it," he said.

Amazingly Jon said, "Yes, Grandpa, you should, in a way. In a way it's your fault. It was what you told me about Indian battles and old arrowheads and spears and tomahawks and old skeletons. But you wouldn't let me go out to look for them. And in the evening, when we all did go out, we never found a single thing. But you said that there were arrowheads all over the farm."

"I said that?" Grandpa asked, amazed. "I said that in so many words?"

Vestri came to Jon's rescue. "Yes, you did, Grandpa. I heard it."

"You certainly managed to give the impression that arrowheads were about as thick as corncobs around here," Grandma agreed. "The other night you were even shouting about having a contest to see who would get the first bushelful of arrowheads."

Grandpa looked astounded. "Did I say that? I certainly did not mean to give the impression that you can pick up the arrowheads the way you pick up apples from the trees. I meant that there

[69]

are a lot of them buried on this farm—for arrowheads. In my lifetime I've maybe found four—five with the one I gave you, Jon. In their lifetimes, my father, his father, and your father, Jon and Vestri, possibly found seven or eight each." He shook his head in surprise at himself. "But even so, Jon, was that any excuse to neglect the puppies?"

Jon shrugged his shoulders and looked uncomfortable. It was hard to explain, and still harder to admit straight out to Grandpa. "Well," he began, "when you wouldn't let me go out to look for arrowheads except for a little while in the evening, I used to sneak out back by the swamp where you couldn't see over the hill, and . . . and . . . then I guess I was looking for arrowheads and forgot about the puppies."

"It looks to me that you and I will have to take turns wearing the hat," Grandpa said. "You for sneaking and doing what was forbidden and me for my loose lip. But I'll tell you what; we'll all go out again tonight, puppies and all, and if we don't find at least one arrowhead, I'll wear that horse's hat, even if I have to wear it to bed."

Jon grinned confusedly. "Okay, Grandpa," he said, "but I guess I'll have to wear it until then." He put the hat on.

Then Grandma got up and took it off Jon's head and hung it back over the door. "I think it's served its purpose," she said. "We all feel better for the hat and for having talked.

Now if you two men will bring a table and chairs, Vestri and I will serve our supper here where it's cool. Then we'll all go out, the four of us and the puppies too, and look for arrow-heads."

Grandpa nodded his head. "The Corncrib Court has come to its end," he said.

7
Last Day

"Today we're going fishing," Grandpa said. "I've promised it ever since the day of the puppies, when you two discovered the swamp and the lake and the heron. It seems that what with the care of the puppies, the heat wave, hunting arrowheads and skeletons, we somehow never got around to going fishing. So it's going to have to be today."

Grandpa was digging worms in the deep, damp barnyard. For some reason Grandpa was wearing the horse's hat. Jon eyed it and began to laugh, but he did not find laughing easy. Something was troubling him. Vestri looked sad and troubled too.

"Are you wearing the horse's hat because we never found any more arrowheads, and now the summer's over?" Jon asked.

Grandfather shook his head. "Nope, it's not for punishment, although it's beginning to look like arrowheads will have to wait until next summer. No, I'm wearing the hat because it's the biggest hat I've got, so it's the biggest protection from the sun. When you're fishing on a low-lying lake down in a swamp between hills, the sun's got a double bite. It catches you downward and then it bounces up again as it reflects from the water."

Grandpa talked so much and dug and dug, Jon had to keep pouncing for the wiggly fast worms and he had no time to think what it was that was bothering him. It was Vestri, standing back doing nothing because she wouldn't touch worms, who finally asked the big question. She really didn't have to ask. Both Jon and Vestri knew. The heat wave was gone and the dog days had gone, but summer was also gone. The summer and the whole summer vacation were over. Yet somehow it foolishly seemed that if you didn't ask about it and if you tried hard not to think about it, it wouldn't be true.

Vestri hesitated, her voice trembling when she finally asked for herself and Jon, "Grandpa, why does it have to be today? Why couldn't we just as well go fishing tomorrow?"

Grandpa kicked his spade deep into the ground, leaned on the long handle, and looked at Jon and Vestri. "Because today is the last day. As you very well know, there has to be an end to every vacation. So Grandma and I picked today.

[73]

My goodness, you'll need a few days to get reacquainted with your mother, and to give her a chance to buy your school clothes and school books, and for you to learn how to behave in town again. So we picked today. Well, we had to pick *some* day!" Then Grandpa dug deep into the soft, moist earth and turned over a spadeful. This time he didn't wait for Jon; he stooped way over to hunt the wiggly worms himself. Jon stooped with him, but he couldn't see the worms—he had tears in his eyes. Vestri looked far away and everybody was very still.

They both had known that one of these days would be the last day of their summer. It was silly that saying it right out made it seem so hard. But Grandpa had said so, and now it was so. This was the last day.

"Can the puppies go along with us, fishing, too?" Jon asked.

"On a last day? They'll be a bother in the boat, but on a last day, you know, anything goes," Grandpa answered.

"Is Grandma going?" Vestri asked. "Oh, here is Grandma," she interrupted herself, surprised. Grandmother must have been listening from someplace in the barn, and now that the sad news had been broken, here she was.

"No, Grandma is not coming," she answered for herself. "I'm just bringing you a picnic fishing-trip lunch. On a last day I like to be alone to do the packing. You know you two bring more truck every summer. I like to spread it all out over the bed and over the whole room before I begin. Then I tuck this here and stuff that there, and, I guess, maybe I tuck in some big hopes for next summer when you'll be back again."

Vestri flew to her and started to hug her, but when Grandma backed away, Vestri said, "Oh, no, I didn't pick up any worms, so my hands aren't messy." Then she hid her face in Grandma's skirt.

Grandma chuckled. "Oh, that reminds me. I put a pair of your gloves in the picnic basket for your fishing. I'm afraid you'll be like me; worms and fish—well, they make you feel queasy, and it goes a bit better with gloves on your hands."

In a muffled voice Vestri said, "I'm not going fishing."

Grandma patted Vestri's head. "Yes, you are," she said firmly. "I think your grandfather thought of the very best thing to do on a last day. There's nothing like fishing—busy fishing—to take your mind off its being the day."

"It'll be busy fishing, all right. Why, there's almost more fish than water in that lake," Grandfather said.

Grandma snorted, Jon hooted, and then suddenly Vestri grinned.

Grandpa grinned too. "Well, with my horse's hat on and my ears sticking through, I can say all kinds of loose words on a last day."

And Jon said, "On a last day anything goes."

[75]

Grandpa went to the barn. When he came out, he had three slender, long cane poles. He put one on Vestri's narrow shoulder and one on Jon's. But the longest, thickest pole he kept for himself.

He let Jon carry the small pail with worms. Grandma looked offended, for he set it right in the picnic basket so Jon could carry it that way. Vestri carried the tackle box. Then Grandpa wrapped a burlap bag around the two oars and his fish pole and threw them across his shoulder.

"Wait a minute. I almost forgot," Grandma said. She hurried to the house and let the puppies out. She certainly wanted to be all alone this day.

"Aren't you taking the truck?" she asked when she came back with Smith, Brown, and Jones trailing behind her.

"Nope!" Grandpa said emphatically. "There's nothing, I've noticed, that smooths out the disturbed soul like a good long walk. Unless maybe it's fishing."

They set out, Grandpa and Vestri and Jon, down the lane to the road and left Grandma behind in the yard. The puppies kept looking back and whining. Then they decided it was more fun to trot after the three moving people.

Jon was walking beside Vestri, not one inch behind, not one inch ahead, and he was eyeing his and Vestri's poles. Then when he'd compared them, he turned so indignantly and so swiftly to Grandpa that he almost knocked the horse's hat from Grandpa's head with the sweeping tip of his pole.

"Grandpa," he said, "you gave Vestri a longer pole than mine. And she's a girl and she doesn't even like fishing and she's afraid of worms and all that, but you gave her a much longer pole."

"Well," Grandpa said impatiently, "that evens things out, doesn't it? Your arms are longer, so you'll be just the same. Anyway, there's enough fish all over that lake—not just at the end of the longest pole." Then Grandfather grinned. "I was wrong," he said. "If there's anything better to smoothen out the sad heart on a last day than a walk, I guess it's a big, envious quarrel."

But Jon's disturbance ended right there, for Grandmother halloed way back from the yard, out from between cupped hands. "Don't stay too long. The bus is coming for them on the dot. Don't forget. . . ."

Grandfather promptly pulled his big watch—he called it a

[77]

turnip—out of his pocket by its leather fob and studied it. "Don't worry, we'll be home in plenty of time," he yelled back. "You just have the frying pan hot and ready."

It was troublesome having three active little dogs in the boat. They skittered and dashed and scrambled under the seats from one end of the boat to the other and back again. They had great fights and quarrels, and they charged the feet of the people with shrill barks and growls. Grandpa had rigged up the lines on Jon and Vestri's poles, and when almost from the first moment they began to catch fish, it became really exciting. The fish flopped and jumped as they landed in the bottom of the boat, and the puppies went all but insane.

Jon and Vestri became so confused at first when their corks shot under water that they pulled their lines up too fast. The fish flew through the air clear over the boat and fell off the lines back into the lake.

Vestri started to cry when she lost her first three fish that way, but Grandfather told her, "Never mind, there's more. Anyway, they went into the lake; you can catch them back again."

The fish were hungry. They bit hard. As soon as a line with the hook and worm dipped under the water, the whole long line and the cork shot down. Vestri pulled up her fourth fish so hard it slapped flat and wet against Grandpa's face and knocked off the horse's hat. Two of the puppies barked wildly after the sailing hat, and Brown, up on one of the seats, almost jumped overboard. Fortunately just then Jon landed a fish and the puppy jumped down to charge it in the bottom of the boat.

Grandpa sat wiping his face with the back of his hand, and at the same time tried to pull in his hat with an oar. Vestri sat dithering on the edge of her seat, wildly anxious to catch her first fish. The one that had slapped Grandpa in the face had fallen back into the water.

"This is how you do it, Vestri," Jon said confidently. "Now watch." But his line shot down so hard, and he snapped it back so nervously that somehow he got the fish smack, slap, wet in his own face.

"Oh, is that how you do it?" Vestri laughed and laughed. She felt much better now.

Suddenly the big blue heron squawked up from behind some reeds at the far end of the lake and flapped away over the hills and the fields to another lake.

"Hear him, Vestri?" Jon said. "He's still laughing at us."

"He thinks we're pretty poor fishermen to be so noisy about it," Grandfather said.

[79]

"Well, we don't need him," Vestri said pertly. She had just landed her first fish very neatly in the bottom of the boat, and it hadn't slapped anyone in the face.

Then with her white gloves, dirty from putting on worms, she managed to get her first twisting fish off the line all by herself.

"Oh, this is so much fun," she said breathlessly. She watched Grandpa put her fish in the burlap sack that hung in the water over the side of the boat to keep the fish fresh and alive.

"Didn't I tell you?" Grandpa asked. He was almost as excited as Vestri, Jon, and the three puppies. "Didn't I tell you there were so many fish in this little lake your arms would get tired from pulling them up?"

"Oh, my arms aren't tired, one bit. I want to catch more and more," Jon said.

"Mine aren't either," Vestri boasted. "This is fun. Grandpa, this is the best thing to do on a last day."

"Well, don't sit there talking about it," Jon said sourly. He on his side of the boat hadn't caught a fish for several minutes, while Grandpa and Vestri had been pulling them in. Just then he had a bite and was too busy to think about last days.

All of a sudden Grandpa had enough of pulling in smallish fish. He told Jon and Vestri he was going to fish down deep where the big fish were—way down on the bottom. He tied another line to the long line already on his pole. He let it down with a great gob of worms on the hook and it drifted slowly away, down and down into the murky deep of the water.

"Oh, I love Grandma," Vestri exclaimed. She had found a second pair of gloves in the basket and she happily drew them on—all white and crisp.

"Girls!" Jon snorted. "Have to fish with gloves!"

They both fussed about the gloves because they had to have something to fuss about. They were jealous of Grandpa fishing for the big fish way down in the deep, mysterious black depths of the swamp lake.

Then they felt better, for they kept catching fish, but nothing happened to Grandpa's line. Grandpa had to sit there, not moving or stirring, not having a thing to do.

The bottom of the burlap bag that hung over the edge of the boat was sinking deeper and deeper with the fish that Jon and Vestri were catching. Vestri's second pair of gloves were already wet and slimy and as dirty as the first pair, but she was too busy to notice. She had another fish for Jon to drop in the sack. They were hard to hold even with gloves on.

They ate their lunch in the boat, for it seemed it would take altogether too much time to pull up anchor, row to shore, and sit on the bank with their picnic. After the fullness of lunch, the heat and the stillness of the afternoon lay over the lake.

Grandpa stretched the white cloth Grandma had used to cover the picnic basket, over the tip of the boat, and the three puppies, worn out from rushing at the splattering fish, fell sound asleep side by side under its protecting shade. Now it was quiet in the boat.

The lake was still, and for a moment neither Jon nor Vestri was even getting a bite. Then Jon nudged Vestri and pointed at Grandpa. He sat nodding on his seat in the heat and the silence. A little wind came over the lake and the boat moved on the ripples to the far end of its anchor rope. And there, right before Jon and Vestri's eyes, down went Grandpa's line! It ripped through the water, then the whole length of it went under and the cork shot out of sight. The long pole, which Grandpa had hooked on to the side of the boat, bowed and bent toward the water. Then the tip of the pole went under, and in the stillness it began to make squeaking, cracking sounds.

Jon and Vestri sat watching it. Nothing moved but Grandpa's line and the bending pole. Grandpa slept on. Suddenly Jon lunged forward as far as he dared and slapped Grandpa's knee with his hand.

Grandpa jerked awake. He jumped up a little, saw the

[82]

water and the lake, and sat down again. Then he saw his shivering, bending pole. He grabbed it, but whatever was down there on the other end of the deep line wouldn't come up no matter how hard Grandpa pulled. The boat moved, but what was down there did not move. Then gradually, gradually, little by little, the tip of the pole came up out of the water. The next moment it ripped down again.

"Grandpa, what is it? What is it?" Vestri gasped. "Grandpa, I'm scared."

Grandpa kept on pulling. "I don't know, Vestri," he said. "I can't see down under the black water any better than you. But whatever it is that's holding my pole is bending it into a hoop. It must be at least an octopus, using all its two hundred arms."

Then Jon knew it was a joke. "Octopuses don't have two hundred arms," he said, giggling. "And they're in the sea, not in lakes."

"Yes, Grandpa. Of course," Vestri agreed, relieved.

"Well, I used the wrong word. I meant a squid," Grandpa said, straining and pulling. "You know those big things with all those arms that even fight whales?"

"Whales are in the sea, too," Vestri said scornfully.

But she clung with both hands to the edge of the seat— her own pole lay forgotten across the boat—and she watched anxiously. Jon clung as hard and watched as anxiously as she. Grandpa's pole still kept coming up and straightening out and then bending down under the water again.

"Ah, now I know. It's the whale himself," Grandpa grunted.

Then, of course, even Vestri knew that Grandpa had just been having fun with them. "It's nothing but a stump on the bottom—or something," she told him.

Just the same it was tense and exciting. Everybody sat still and stared into the deep water to see what would come up. Even the puppies woke up; it must have been from the quiet. Without a bark or a wave from their little tails, they stretched up against the side of the boat and peered over the edge at Grandfather's squeaking, swishing pole in the water.

At last out of the murk something big and shadowy came up at the end of the straining line. They began to see the shadowy shape. It sank away again, then came up once more as Grandfather pulled steadily. Now he pulled the pole in, laid it across the boat, and then began to pull the line in, hand over hand.

Jon and Vestri could hardly breathe; it was so tense and scary, yet so impossible to wait another minute to find out what was coming up from the depths of the lake. Then it broke surface. It was a tree—a whole little tree—about as thick

[84]

as an arm, Grandpa's arm, but many-branched and sprawly. Grandpa dragged it toward the boat so he could get hold of it to pull his hook out of the branch.

Suddenly Jon jumped right up in the boat. Vestri pulled him back, but Jon didn't even know she was pulling. "Grandpa, Grandpa," he screamed, and pointed. "It's an ax head. It's an Indian ax head! Your line is caught around an ax head!"

Grandfather leaned out over the edge of the boat and said, "Why, so it is. You're right. Your eyes are better than mine. It's an ax head driven deep into that branch."

Grandfather reached down and lifted the tree from the water by the ax head. But even then it didn't let go. He had to lay the little tree across the prow of the boat, and wrench and pry at the ax head with both hands before it would let go.

"Well, well," he said. "That long-ago Indian must have been real mad at something. He really drove that ax into that tree. The thongs rotted away under the water, and the ax handle came to the surface and floated away. But the tree held that ax from the day the Indian drove it into it and it fell into the water.

"Man," Grandpa said. "Maybe that Indian had just driven his ax into the tree and when he turned around—there stood a mastodon. Boy, did he take off without waiting. Maybe the

[85]

mastodon rammed the tree into the lake and it floated away, and long afterward it became water-logged and sank to the bottom. And there it's stayed until this minute."

"Grandpa, stop!" Vestri begged. "Or you'll get Jon so excited I won't be able to hold him—he'll jump out of the boat."

Grandpa laughed. He finally had the ax head loose, and with a flourish he swept off the horse's hat and handed the ax head to Jon. Then he threw the tree overboard, and threw the horse's hat after it. "I sure don't need that hat anymore. Not when I've come across with a flint ax head, and a big one at that. . . . Man, all I promised was a measly little old arrowhead. And now you have an ax head. And now *my* head is too big for a horse's hat."

Jon didn't laugh; he sat there sort of stunned, bent over, holding the wet, crusted ax head against him. It was such a marvelous thing that he could find no words.

Vestri and Grandpa looked at the old tree drifting slowly down into the dark murk it had come from. At last it was only a shadow, and then it was gone.

Jon clutched the ax head as if it were a jewel. Then he said in a small voice, "Grandpa, I don't want to fish anymore. Oh, it was a great day, and now I don't want to fish anymore."

Vestri looked at Jon. That was a strange thing to say, but

[86]

Grandpa nodded his head. He picked up the oars. "Wind up the lines around your poles," he said. "Jon is right: When it's perfect, then it's time to go home."

"Thank you, Grandpa," Jon whispered.

After him, Vestri said, "Thank you, Grandpa, for a great day."

8

Puppy Summer

They walked through the swamp grass down the narrow path
that led away from the lake. Grandfather walked ahead with
all the fishing poles and the oars on his shoulder, and the
dripping sack with the fish hanging from the end of the oars.
Jon and Vestri, carrying the picnic basket, followed well behind the dripping sack. The three puppies were inside the
basket, because with his very first steps on the raised path
little Jones had almost fallen off it into a black, swampy hole.
Vestri was terrified that Jones or one of the other puppies
would disappear in a bottomless hole in the swamp.

"Just like your giant skeleton," she told Jon. She wasn't
joking; she was scared. She kept an eye on the three bobbing
heads of the puppies in the basket, lest they jump out.

Away from the lake, around a turn in the path, deep among

the high, dark huckleberry bushes, stood something. At first Jon and Vestri thought it was the heron half hidden by the bushes, then to their delight it turned out to be Grandma. Grandma had come to get them. She was worried. "What time is it?" she asked Grandpa. "Have you any idea what time it is? Have you been watching the time?"

"Oh, we had fun, Grandma . . . and look, Grandma," Jon shouted. He dug into the basket for the ax head, but he couldn't find it in his haste. Grandma was too worried to pay any attention.

"I guess we did have fun," Grandpa said. "I sure never thought of the time." He pulled out his watch and peered at it. "The turnip says . . . oh, no! Where did the time go? The turnip says almost three o'clock. We've got to hurry now or we won't be ready when that bus stops at our house."

Jon squirmed by Grandpa on the narrow path, almost knocking the watch out of his hand, and ran to Grandma to show her the ax head. "Imagine, Grandma," he shouted. "Imagine! We go fishing on our last day and we find a real, genuine, flint, Indian ax head. Look how big it is. Grandpa caught it on his hook. It came from the bottom of the lake, and it's way back from the time of the mastodons."

Grandmother shook her head and made surprised sounds. She stared at the ax head, but she was still nervous. "It's wonderful, Jon, wonderful, but we've really got to hurry. . . . Oh,

I'm glad you've got the puppies in the basket. Then at least
they won't hold us up. Jon, you help me with the basket,
and we'll carry the puppies home. Give Vestri your ax head."

Jon wouldn't hear of it. The ax head had to go in the basket
with the puppies, the dishes, and the used towels. He had to
carry it himself. Vestri walked behind the basket to see that
none of the puppies would topple out.

Grandma was in such a hurry, she and Jon led the way
down the path through the rest of the swamp. "That bus is
going to stop at the end of our lane just especially for you,"

Grandmother said. "So we certainly must be ready in time. . . . Oh, you had me worried! I packed the bags, had lunch, straightened out the house, and got myself calmed a bit, and still you weren't back. And then I noticed that the clock had stopped. It would stop on this day—of all days. And the old alarm clock hasn't run since I used it to mother the puppies. Well, I finally got myself in such a state, I took off for the lake. I figured no one would watch the time—not if the fish were biting."

Jon had not heard a word of all of Grandmother's talk, because he answered her by saying, "Imagine, going fishing and getting a real Indian ax head. Oh, Grandma, it's been a great day."

Behind Grandma and Jon, Grandpa and Vestri looked at each other and grinned. "Those two are side by side, but they're right now in two different worlds," Grandpa said softly. Then aloud he said to Grandma, "Now calm yourself, and stop your fussing. There's plenty of time. You just got yourself worked up because the clock stopped. When we get home, I'll fix the fish while these two get busy getting themselves scrubbed and dressed. We can't be having them smell like a couple of fish peddlers on that bus. But for all that, we're still going to take time to have a fish fry. I can't think of a better good-bye than a fish fry. That bus doesn't come until seven."

"Then can we have the fish fry in the corncrib?" Vestri begged. "That would be fun—oh, that would be nice—a good-bye meal in the corncrib."

"If you hurry. If we all hurry we can do everything," Grandma said.

Tired and hot, thirsty and dusty, and a little forlorn, they hustled down the long lane toward home. Grandpa threw down the fish poles and oars, gave a hasty spank first to Jon and then to Vestri, and ordered: "Now you two hurry and clean up. No fooling around! I'll clean the fish, Grandma will fry them—and by the time you're washed we'll be ready for the fish fry. The bus driver is going to stop right at our lane as a special favor to me, so we won't have to wait around that dreary little bus station. If there's anything I hate, it's waiting at stations with nothing to do but feel bad."

Jon and Vestri ran. But just to make sure that Jon would really get bathed and dressed, Grandpa ran after him and took the flint ax head out of his hand. "Don't worry. It'll be beside your plate—I'll clean it up a bit when I clean the fish. But if we're late for the bus on account of you dreaming of ax heads, I swear I'll walk all the way back to the lake and throw that ax head back where it came from."

"Yes, yes," Grandma said. "Please hurry now—no fooling and no dreaming."

[93]

It was over. The hurrying, the bathing, the scrubbing, the dressing, even the fish fry and the last meal. There stood the three bags just outside the corncrib. Grandfather looked at the bags, then at the four fish left lying on the platter, sighed, wiped his mouth, and jumped up.

"There's no time to wash up," Grandma said. She reached over the table and wiped Jon's and Vestri's faces. She made them rub their fishy hands hard with the same soapy washcloth.

The three puppies were sound asleep in a corner, and everyone tried to tiptoe away so as not to wake them. But they didn't dare to close the door—it squeaked too much.

"It'll be easier for you with the pups not along," Grandpa whispered.

Grandfather carried the two smaller bags, and Grandma and Jon carried the big one between them. Vestri carried the precious flint ax head. But she had to walk behind Grandpa and ahead of Jon so Jon could keep an eye on her. "Don't you drop it," he warned.

"Oh, Jon," Grandmother said.

"Takes after his grandmother," Grandpa said.

Then no one said anything more. But Vestri giggled.

It wasn't until they set the bags down in the grass by the side of the road that they saw the three puppies. The little dogs had come quietly, sleepily, on behind all the way down the lane. Now they stood confused and questioning, their little tails wagging vaguely. And then . . . then it was as if with the setting down of the suitcases and the puppies so quiet—that that had made the end come. In that moment the great day—the excitement of the fishing and of finding the ax head and having the fish fry—was all gone. Instead, in its place, the end had come.

Vestri stood looking at the puppies, and suddenly she was crying. "It isn't fair," she wept. "It isn't fair."

To cut her crying short, Grandfather asked sternly, "What isn't fair?"

Maybe Vestri didn't even know what she had said, because she looked at Grandfather in bewilderment.

Jon came to her rescue. "I guess she means . . . Well, things aren't fair," he said hesitantly, sadly. He swallowed a couple of times.

"But life is life and it has to be lived—whatever it brings," Grandfather said. "Some days it brings puppies, and some days it brings a bus that ends a vacation and a whole summer and takes us back to school. Still, we certainly had a full summer, but an end comes and this is our summer's end."

"But it *isn't* fair," Vestri insisted. "It isn't fair. We've just had the puppies a couple of weeks, and now we've got to go home."

"Vestri," Grandmother said reproachfully. "But wasn't it

wonderful to have your little puppy summer still come at the end of the long summer before you had to go back to school?"

"Yes," Vestri sobbed, "but now just when Smith is becoming Smith, and Brown is Brown, and Jones is Jones, and they're not just little puppies anymore—now we have to go home. Why, I can tell Smith from Brown, and Brown from Jones, even if I just hear them—I don't have to see them. But we had them such a short time! There was the whole, long summer, but we had them only a couple of weeks."

"Well, exactly," said Grandfather. "It's as your grandmother said; that was your extra, little puppy summer, added on to the long one. And wasn't it better than not having the puppies at all?"

"But, Grandpa," Jon argued along with Vestri. "We hardly had them at all, and now we have to go back home to school. All we have in the city is Mother and the apartment and school, and Mother is gone to work all day. Here we have you and Grandma, and the three puppies. But if we come back next summer, Smith, Brown, and Jones won't be puppies anymore. They'll be grown dogs."

"Come to think of it," Grandpa said, "neither will you two be puppies anymore. Life is like that. . . . Remember last year when we put you on the bus to go home? Grandma hung tags on the two of you. She didn't even think of it this summer. And last summer did I take you fishing as I did today?

Who knows, by the end of next summer I may let you go fishing alone. Who knows? This may very well be *your* last puppy summer."

Jon looked at Vestri and Vestri looked at Jon, then Vestri said doubtfully, "Next year our puppies won't be puppies anymore, and they won't even know us."

"Of course next year they won't be puppies. And neither will you. But they'll be here—Smith, Brown, and Jones— when you come for your long summer vacation. Can't you see them? There you two come up the lane walking lopsided from the weight of your satchels. And when you're about halfway up the lane there'll come this bark from behind our farmyard gate. It's a short bark that says, 'I don't quite recognize you, strangers. Advance and be recognized. But come slowly, come carefully.' That'll be your this-year's puppy Smith.

"Right after that will come a second bark. That'll be Brown, I guess, but full-size now and become a dog since you two saw him last. And his bark says, 'I don't quite recognize the size and the long legs, and the big, long steps, but still, there's something about you, boy, and about you, girl, that I seem to know. Something about the looks, something about the smell. . . . Come closer, please. I bark, but I don't bite.'

"Then the third puppy, now a big dog—he used to be little Jones—comes out with a coughing, long bark. But he

[97]

doesn't bark at the boy and the girl struggling with their big suitcases up the long lane. He barks a coughing bark, because there is no question in it. He's barking at the other dogs and he's saying, 'What's the matter with you, Smith? What's wrong with your stupid head, Brown? Can't you remember? Don't you recognize them? Why, that's Vestri and Jon come back to us, and there's a whole, long summer before us again.' "

Vestri had been listening to Grandfather in such rapture her mouth had kept moving as she formed the words right along with him. Jon's mouth, too, was open with delight. Then Vestri flew straight at Grandpa, she threw herself at him. "Oh, Grandpa, I love you," she sighed.

Jon flew to Grandma. Then both he and Vestri almost at the same time whirled around and Jon flung himself at Grandpa, and Grandma had to hold Vestri tight.

And then—none of them heard it come—there was the bus. It drew up with a squeak of tires in a spray of gravel. Everybody rushed to grab up the puppies that weren't used to roads and cars and buses.

The door of the bus rammed open, and the driver shouted down, "You two kids up here on the double while I toss your baggage aboard. I went fishing today, so I'm late. Get your-selves in this bus on the double."

Jon and Vestri obediently rushed up the steps. They passed

the driver coming down and Jon told him, "So did we go fishing today. See what we caught?" He proudly held up his Indian ax head.

The driver glanced at it over his shoulder. As he jumped down he said, "My gosh—now don't tell me—a petrified fish!"

Grandfather helped the driver with the luggage. In a moment the driver came racing back up the steps of the bus,

but before the air pressure door could close, Grandpa shouted, " 'Bye, Vestri. 'Bye, Jon."

Grandma, at the roadside, made an O of her mouth and kissed the bundle of puppies she held in her arms, each one in turn—Smith, Brown, and Jones—right on their little flat heads, for Jon and Vestri.

Then with a roar of the motor and a great backward spurting of gravel, they were on their way. The end of their summer had come. All that was left was a quick hand wave and a blown kiss, and the long shout that Vestri and Jon shouted together out of the back window: " 'Bye, Grandpa. 'Bye, Grandma. 'Bye, Smith, Brown, and Jones. See you next summer. See you next summer."

For that is what there still was—the whole, big, next summer.